TALES FROM MAD LIBS

NIGHTMARE AT CAMP Smelly LAKE

ADJECTIVE

BY BETSY NIGHTWOOD

MAD LIBS
An Imprint of Penguin Random House LLC, New York

Mad Libs format and text copyright © 2019 by Penguin Random House LLC. All rights reserved.

Concept created by Roger Price & Leonard Stern

Cover illustration by Scott Brooks

Published by Mad Libs,
an imprint of Penguin Random House LLC, New York.
Printed in the USA.

Visit us online at www.penguinrandomhouse.com.

ISBN 9781524792145
3 5 7 9 10 8 6 4 2

INSTRUCTIONS

MAD LIBS® is a game for people who don't like games!
It can be played by one, two, three, four, or forty.

• RIDICULOUSLY SIMPLE DIRECTIONS

In this book you will find a story containing blank spaces where words are
left out. One player, the READER, asks the other players, the WRITERS, to
give him/her words. These words are used to fill in the blank spaces in the
story.

• TO PLAY

The READER asks each WRITER in turn to call out a word—an adjective or
a noun or whatever the space calls for and uses them to fill in the blank
spaces in the story. The result is a MAD LIBS® game.

When the READER then reads the completed MAD LIBS® game to the other
players, they will discover that they have written a story that is fantastic,
screamingly funny, shocking, silly, crazy, or just plain dumb—depending
upon which words each WRITER called out.

• EXAMPLE (*Before* and *After*)

" _____ !" he said _____
        EXCLAMATION   ADVERB

as he jumped into his convertible _____ and
                                                              NOUN

drove off with his _____ wife.
                          ADJECTIVE

" _____OUCH_____ !" he said _____STUPIDLY_____
        EXCLAMATION   ADVERB

as he jumped into his convertible _____CAT_____ and
                                                              NOUN

drove off with his _____BRAVE_____ wife.
                          ADJECTIVE

MAD☺LIBS®

QUICK REVIEW

In case you have forgotten what adjectives, adverbs, nouns, and verbs are, here is a quick review:

An ADJECTIVE describes something or somebody. *Lumpy, soft, ugly, messy,* and *short* are adjectives.

An ADVERB tells how something is done. It modifies a verb and usually ends in "ly." *Modestly, stupidly, greedily,* and *carefully* are adverbs.

A NOUN is the name of a person, place, or thing. *Sidewalk, umbrella, bridle, bathtub,* and *nose* are nouns.

A VERB is an action word. *Run, pitch, jump,* and *swim* are verbs. Put the verbs in past tense if the directions say PAST TENSE. *Ran, pitched, jumped,* and *swam* are verbs in the past tense.

When we ask for A PLACE, we mean any sort of place: a country or city (*Spain, Cleveland*) or a room (*bathroom, kitchen*).

An EXCLAMATION or SILLY WORD is any sort of funny sound, gasp, grunt, or outcry, like *Wow!, Ouch!, Whomp!, Ick!,* and *Gadzooks!*

When we ask for specific words, like a NUMBER, a COLOR, an ANIMAL, or a PART OF THE BODY, we mean a word that is one of those things, like *seven, blue, horse,* or *head.*

When we ask for a PLURAL, it means more than one. For example, *cat* pluralized is *cats.*

MAD LIBS® is fun to play with friends, but you can also play it by yourself! To begin with, DO NOT look at the chapter on the next page. Fill in the blanks on this page with the words called for. Then, using the words you have selected, fill in the blank spaces in the chapter.

Now you've created your own hilarious MAD LIBS® game!

CHAPTER 1: FIRST DAY OF CAMP, SUMMER 1981

NOUN _____

ADVERB _____

PERSON IN ROOM _____

ADJECTIVE _____

VERB _____

NOUN _____

ADJECTIVE _____

NUMBER _____

SAME PERSON IN ROOM _____

ANIMAL _____

VERB _____

VERB ENDING IN "ING" _____

EXCLAMATION _____

VERB (PAST TENSE) _____

ADVERB _____

PLURAL NOUN _____

NOUN _____

CHAPTER 1:
FIRST DAY OF CAMP, SUMMER 1981

It was a clear summer day, and the _____ was shining
                                    NOUN

_____ in the sky. A first-year camper named _____
ADVERB   PERSON IN ROOM

was floating on a raft in Camp _____ Lake. Suddenly, the
                                 ADJECTIVE

water began to _____ and smell like a/an _____.
                 VERB   NOUN

Something slimy and _____ smacked the camper in the face.
                      ADJECTIVE

"How weird," the camper said as a creature with _____ eyes
                                                    NUMBER

burst through the water!

_____ screamed like a frightened _____, but
SAME PERSON IN ROOM   ANIMAL

no one could _____ the screams. The creature wasted no
                VERB

time _____ its teeth into the camper's skin!
       VERB ENDING IN "ING"

"_____!" said the camper, but the creature would not
   EXCLAMATION

let go.

The raft flipped over and the camper _____ from
                                        VERB (PAST TENSE)

sight. The lake grew _____ quiet. When _____
                       ADVERB   PLURAL NOUN

finally arrived on the scene, all that remained was the camper's bucket

hat floating on the surface of the _____.
                                     NOUN

MAD LIBS® is fun to play with friends, but you can also play it by yourself! To begin with, DO NOT look at the chapter on the next page. Fill in the blanks on this page with the words called for. Then, using the words you have selected, fill in the blank spaces in the chapter.

Now you've created your own hilarious MAD LIBS® game!

CHAPTER 2:
FIRST DAY OF CAMP, THE PRESENT

ADJECTIVE _____

COLOR _____

ARTICLE OF CLOTHING (PLURAL) _____

ANIMAL (PLURAL) _____

FIRST NAME _____

PART OF THE BODY (PLURAL) _____

NOUN _____

SILLY WORD _____

ADJECTIVE _____

VERB _____

ADVERB _____

PLURAL NOUN _____

PLURAL NOUN _____

PART OF THE BODY _____

VERB _____

ARTICLE OF CLOTHING _____

NUMBER _____

CHAPTER 2:
FIRST DAY OF CAMP, THE PRESENT

"All aboard the _____ express!" a counselor with _____
<u>ADJECTIVE</u>   <u>COLOR</u>

hair shouted. "Second-year campers must enter the bus wearing their

_____ backward. Only permission slips signed
<u>ARTICLE OF CLOTHING (PLURAL)</u>

by pet _____ or Uncle _____ are valid."
       <u>ANIMAL (PLURAL)</u>   <u>FIRST NAME</u>

Natasha and Leon rolled their _____ as they
                              <u>PART OF THE BODY (PLURAL)</u>

boarded the bus. This was their second _____ at Camp
                                        <u>NOUN</u>

_____ Lake. They knew how _____ the counselors could be.
<u>SILLY WORD</u>   <u>ADJECTIVE</u>

"Actually, we'll _____ onto the bus however we like, thank
                <u>VERB</u>

you _____ much," Natasha muttered.
    <u>ADVERB</u>

She and Leon found a seat in the back of the bus where all the cool

_____ sat.
<u>PLURAL NOUN</u>

"Now, let the _____ begin!" the counselor shouted into a
             <u>PLURAL NOUN</u>

megaphone. Globs of spit flew from his _____.
                                       <u>PART OF THE BODY</u>

"Say it, don't _____ it!" Leon whispered, wiping saliva off of
              <u>VERB</u>

his _____.
    <u>ARTICLE OF CLOTHING</u>

"Listen up, folks!" the counselor continued. "_____ miles until
                                               <u>NUMBER</u>

we reach the camp!"

MAD LIBS® is fun to play with friends, but you can also play it by yourself! To begin with, DO NOT look at the chapter on the next page. Fill in the blanks on this page with the words called for. Then, using the words you have selected, fill in the blank spaces in the chapter.

Now you've created your own hilarious MAD LIBS® game!

CHAPTER 3:
GREASED WATERMELON POLO

VERB _____

PERSON IN ROOM _____

PART OF THE BODY (PLURAL) _____

VERB _____

ADVERB _____

TYPE OF LIQUID _____

VERB _____

NOUN _____

NOUN _____

VERB _____

ANIMAL (PLURAL) _____

VERB _____

COLOR _____

ADJECTIVE _____

NOUN _____

ADVERB _____

CHAPTER 3:
GREASED WATERMELON POLO

"Campers! It's time to _____ a game of greased watermelon
                              VERB

polo," Counselor _____ announced.
                 PERSON IN ROOM

Natasha and Leon snapped their gum and crossed their

_____ . "Can we _____ to our cabins first?"
PART OF THE BODY (PLURAL)   VERB

Natasha asked. "The heat is _____ killing me!"
                            ADVERB

"Sorry, campers," the counselor replied. "You'll have to grease your

watermelons with slippery _____ and _____ in
                          TYPE OF LIQUID   VERB

the lake before reporting to your bunks!" The teenage campers did as

they were told and jumped in the _____ with slippery melons.
                                  NOUN

"Okay, campers," the counselor started. "The _____ of the
                                             NOUN

game is to _____ your melon to the opposite side of the lake.
           VERB

Watch out for _____! They can _____ underwater."
              ANIMAL (PLURAL)   VERB

Suddenly, the lake turned fluorescent _____ . Campers
                                      COLOR

screamed and splashed in fear. "What's going on?" Leon asked. "And

what is that _____ smell?"
             ADJECTIVE

"Everybody out of the _____!" the counselor screamed.
                      NOUN

"Dry off and report to your cabins _____!"
                                   ADVERB

MAD LIBS® is fun to play with friends, but you can also play it by yourself! To begin with, DO NOT look at the chapter on the next page. Fill in the blanks on this page with the words called for. Then, using the words you have selected, fill in the blank spaces in the chapter.

Now you've created your own hilarious MAD LIBS® game!

CHAPTER 4:
MESS HALL RUMORS

ANIMAL _____

VERB (PAST TENSE) _____

ADJECTIVE _____

VERB _____

NOUN _____

SAME ANIMAL _____

FIRST NAME _____

TYPE OF FOOD (PLURAL) _____

ADJECTIVE _____

ADJECTIVE _____

NOUN _____

VERB _____

PART OF THE BODY _____

PERSON IN ROOM _____

EXCLAMATION _____

PLURAL NOUN _____

VERB _____

CHAPTER 4:
MESS HALL RUMORS

"I still smell like a/an _____," Natasha complained as the

ANIMAL

campers _____ to the mess hall for dinner. After the

VERB (PAST TENSE)

_____ pond incident, the counselors made all of the campers

ADJECTIVE

shower and _____ their bodies with a stiff bar of _____.

VERB   NOUN

"I'm definitely as *hungry* as a/an _____," Leon replied.

SAME ANIMAL

Down in the mess hall, Lunch Lady _____ served hot

FIRST NAME

_____ with a/an _____ spatula. The lunch lady

TYPE OF FOOD (PLURAL)   ADJECTIVE

plopped _____ food on Leon's plate. "This smells like rotting

ADJECTIVE

_____," Leon mumbled.

NOUN

"Take it or _____ it," the lunch lady said. The rest of the

VERB

campers shuffled through the line, gossiping.

"I heard that under the lunch lady's hairnet is a third _____

PART OF THE BODY

that she uses to curse people," Natasha whispered.

"Watch it," said _____. "The lunch lady hears

PERSON IN ROOM

everything."

"_____!" the lunch lady bellowed. The campers ate their

EXCLAMATION

_____ in silence. No one dared to _____ for seconds.

PLURAL NOUN   VERB

MAD LIBS® is fun to play with friends, but you can also play it by yourself! To begin with, DO NOT look at the chapter on the next page. Fill in the blanks on this page with the words called for. Then, using the words you have selected, fill in the blank spaces in the chapter.

Now you've created your own hilarious MAD LIBS® game!

CHAPTER 5:
CAMPFIRE STORIES

NUMBER _____

NOUN _____

FIRST NAME _____

ADJECTIVE _____

ANIMAL _____

ADVERB _____

COLOR _____

PART OF THE BODY (PLURAL) _____

ADJECTIVE _____

ADVERB _____

LAST NAME _____

PLURAL NOUN _____

PART OF THE BODY _____

ADJECTIVE _____

NUMBER _____

CHAPTER 5:
CAMPFIRE STORIES

Later that night, at _____ o'clock, the campers gathered for
        NUMBER

spooky _____ stories by the campfire. Counselor _____
        NOUN   _FIRST NAME_

was just ending a particularly _____ tale.
                               ADJECTIVE

"The last time we saw the ghost _____, it was on the
                                ANIMAL

basketball courts at midnight," said the counselor. "It stared at us

_____, its _____ eyes blazing . . ."
ADVERB   _COLOR_

Crack! A hush fell across the fire. The campers craned their

_____ toward the sound. A/An _____ figure
PART OF THE BODY (PLURAL)   _ADJECTIVE_

stood hunched by the woodshed across from the campfire. The figure

turned and stared _____ at the campers.
                  ADVERB

"Looks like yeh need some more wood on the fire," the figure said.

"Good thinking, Groundskeeper _____!" the counselor
                              LAST NAME

replied to the shadowy figure. The groundskeeper dumped more

_____ onto the fire and propped his _____
PLURAL NOUN   _PART OF THE BODY_

on a bench next to a/an _____ camper named Wanda.
                        ADJECTIVE

"If you kiddos wanna hear a scary story, yeh shoulda been here 'bout

_____ years ago . . ."
NUMBER

MAD LIBS® is fun to play with friends, but you can also play it by yourself! To begin with, DO NOT look at the chapter on the next page. Fill in the blanks on this page with the words called for. Then, using the words you have selected, fill in the blank spaces in the chapter.

Now you've created your own hilarious MAD LIBS® game!

CHAPTER 6:
THE SAD TALE OF AMANDA

VERB _____

PLURAL NOUN _____

ADJECTIVE _____

PERSON IN ROOM _____

ADJECTIVE _____

ANIMAL _____

ADJECTIVE _____

ADJECTIVE _____

COLOR _____

EXCLAMATION _____

ADJECTIVE _____

ADJECTIVE _____

NOUN _____

CHAPTER 6:
THE SAD TALE OF AMANDA

"_____ us the story," Wanda said with a grin. The fire
____VERB____

crackled and cast shadows on the _____.
_____PLURAL NOUN

"Well," the old man began, "it was in all the newspapers: Missing

Camper and _____ Creature on the Loose!"
_____ADJECTIVE

"That's enough," Counselor _____ warned. But the old
_____PERSON IN ROOM

man ignored the counselor and continued.

"Amanda disappeared in 1981. They never could figure out what

_____ thing took 'er away . . ."
___ADJECTIVE

"Was it a/an _____?" Wanda asked.
_____ANIMAL

"Nah," said the groundskeeper. "It was _____ and slimy.
_____ADJECTIVE

And it came from near the _____ burial grounds!"
_____ADJECTIVE

Hsssssssssssssss. The campfire turned _____ and went dark.
_____COLOR

The campers screamed in unison, "_____!"
_____EXCLAMATION

Leon and Natasha held each other for _____ life! Footsteps
_____ADJECTIVE

echoed through the woods, followed by a/an _____ scream,
_____ADJECTIVE

and then silence. The old groundskeeper lit a/an _____.
_____NOUN

"Wanda is gone!" someone yelled.

From TALES FROM MAD LIBS®: NIGHTMARE AT CAMP SMELLY LAKE
Copyright © 2019 by Penguin Random House LLC.

MAD LIBS® is fun to play with friends, but you can also play it by yourself! To begin with, DO NOT look at the chapter on the next page. Fill in the blanks on this page with the words called for. Then, using the words you have selected, fill in the blank spaces in the chapter.

Now you've created your own hilarious MAD LIBS® game!

CHAPTER 7:
WANDA HAS VANISHED!

ADVERB _____

ADJECTIVE _____

ADJECTIVE _____

NUMBER _____

COLOR _____

SILLY WORD _____

VERB _____

ADJECTIVE _____

ADJECTIVE _____

VERB _____

PART OF THE BODY (PLURAL) _____

COLOR _____

VERB ENDING IN "ING" _____

CHAPTER 7:
WANDA HAS VANISHED!

"Wanda is gone!" Leon screamed _____.
_____ADVERB_____

"Hope she doesn't end up like _____ little Amanda,"
_____ADJECTIVE_____

mumbled the groundskeeper.

Suddenly, a stampede of counselors rushed toward the _____
_____ADJECTIVE_____

campfire. All _____ of the counselors wore matching _____
_____NUMBER_____COLOR

bucket hats. "Never fear! The Camp _____ Lake Safety Squad
_____SILLY WORD_____

is here!" they said in unison.

Leon ran toward the counselors. "Shouldn't we pick up the phone

and _____ 9-1-1?" he pleaded.
_____VERB_____

But a counselor silenced the _____ camper. "I'm sure this is
_____ADJECTIVE_____

just a/an _____ prank," said the counselor. "We'll handle it
_____ADJECTIVE_____

ourselves. Everybody, please _____ back to your cabins! Now!"
_____VERB_____

All of the counselors pressed their _____ to their
_____PART OF THE BODY (PLURAL)_____

foreheads at the same time. Something under their bucket hats glowed

bright _____. "What the heck is that?!" Natasha whispered,
_____COLOR_____

_____ with fear.
___VERB ENDING IN "ING"___

"C'mon, kids," the groundskeeper muttered. "Let's head back."

From TALES FROM MAD LIBS®: NIGHTMARE AT CAMP SMELLY LAKE
Copyright © 2019 by Penguin Random House LLC.

MAD LIBS® is fun to play with friends, but you can also play it by yourself! To begin with, DO NOT look at the chapter on the next page. Fill in the blanks on this page with the words called for. Then, using the words you have selected, fill in the blank spaces in the chapter.

Now you've created your own hilarious MAD LIBS® game!

CHAPTER 8:
THINGS THAT GO THUMP IN THE NIGHT

PLURAL NOUN _____

ANIMAL _____

VERB _____

ADJECTIVE _____

VERB _____

TYPE OF LIQUID _____

NOUN _____

PERSON IN ROOM _____

ADJECTIVE _____

SILLY WORD _____

VERB _____

ADJECTIVE _____

VERB ENDING IN "ING" _____

PLURAL NOUN _____

CHAPTER 8:
THINGS THAT GO THUMP IN THE NIGHT

Back at the cabin, Leon and Natasha plopped onto their _____.
                                                    PLURAL NOUN

"I hope Wanda wasn't eaten by a/an _____ or something,"
                                        ANIMAL

Leon whispered.

"Yeah," said Natasha. "Just because she was unpopular doesn't mean

she should _____!" *THUD!*
                VERB

Natasha looked up and saw a/an _____ tentacle _____
                                   ADJECTIVE   VERB

against the cabin window. The tentacle slid down the glass pane, leaving

a trail of _____. "What the _____ is that?" Leon squealed.
          TYPE OF LIQUID   NOUN

"Attention, campers," a counselor named _____ said over
                                         PERSON IN ROOM

the cabin's intercom. "There seem to be some _____ disturbances
                                              ADJECTIVE

this evening. Never fear. The Camp _____ Safety Squad is here!"
                                    SILLY WORD

"Well, where are they now?!" Leon wailed.

"Just try to _____ if you can, I guess," said Natasha. "I'm sure
             VERB

everything will be _____ in the morning."
                   ADJECTIVE

Out the window, Leon saw a Safety Squad counselor running toward

the hills. "She's _____ toward the ancient burial
                 VERB ENDING IN "ING"

_____," Leon whispered. "Just like the groundskeeper said . . ."
PLURAL NOUN

MAD LIBS® is fun to play with friends, but you can also play it by yourself! To begin with, DO NOT look at the chapter on the next page. Fill in the blanks on this page with the words called for. Then, using the words you have selected, fill in the blank spaces in the chapter.

Now you've created your own hilarious MAD LIBS® game!

CHAPTER 9:
WANDA RETURNS

PART OF THE BODY _____

VERB (PAST TENSE) _____

TYPE OF FOOD _____

PART OF THE BODY _____

ADJECTIVE _____

TYPE OF BUILDING _____

NUMBER _____

ADVERB _____

ADJECTIVE _____

VERB ENDING IN "ING" _____

NOUN _____

VERB _____

NOUN _____

ADJECTIVE _____

ANIMAL _____

PART OF THE BODY _____

CHAPTER 9:
WANDA RETURNS

"Wake up," Wanda said, slapping Natasha's _____.
PART OF THE BODY

Natasha _____ and rolled over in her bunk. "I don't want
VERB (PAST TENSE)

that nasty _____, Lunch Lady," Natasha said in her sleep.
TYPE OF FOOD

Wanda tapped Leon's _____ next and he startled awake.
PART OF THE BODY

"Wanda?" he gasped, looking at the _____ girl. "How did you
ADJECTIVE

get into our _____? Aren't there, like, _____ people
TYPE OF BUILDING NUMBER

looking for you?" Wanda coughed _____, waking Natasha.
ADVERB

"What happened?" asked a very _____ Natasha. She looked
ADJECTIVE

at the strange girl _____ next to her bunk. "Wanda!
VERB ENDING IN "ING"

You scared the _____ out of me!"
NOUN

"Help me, please!" the girl said. "The counselors aren't what they

_____ they are. They're all—"
VERB

But the _____ to the cabin swung open and a Safety Squad
NOUN

counselor stepped inside. "Wanda!" the counselor said with a/an

_____ smile. "You can't be around campers now that you have
ADJECTIVE

_____ flu." With that, he snatched Wanda up by her
ANIMAL

_____ and whisked her out the door.
PART OF THE BODY

MAD LIBS® is fun to play with friends, but you can also play it by yourself! To begin with, DO NOT look at the chapter on the next page. Fill in the blanks on this page with the words called for. Then, using the words you have selected, fill in the blank spaces in the chapter.

Now you've created your own hilarious MAD LIBS® game!

CHAPTER 10:
SAFETY SQUAD FRAUD

NOUN _____

PART OF THE BODY _____

TYPE OF FOOD (PLURAL) _____

ADJECTIVE _____

NOUN _____

PART OF THE BODY _____

EXCLAMATION _____

PART OF THE BODY (PLURAL) _____

VERB _____

ADJECTIVE _____

ANIMAL _____

PLURAL NOUN _____

ADJECTIVE _____

TYPE OF FOOD (PLURAL) _____

NOUN _____

CHAPTER 10:
SAFETY SQUAD FRAUD

Natasha and Leon hurried to the _____ to spy on the
<u>NOUN</u>

counselor and Wanda. The counselor had Wanda thrown over his

_____ like a sack of _____.
PART OF THE BODY   TYPE OF FOOD (PLURAL)

"Let's get you back to the Medical Ward, Wanda," said the counselor.

"We think you could be _____ and highly contagious!" They
ADJECTIVE

watched as the counselor stopped by the entrance of the _____.
NOUN

He lifted up his hat to reveal a glowing third _____!
PART OF THE BODY

Leon and Natasha screamed, "_____!" then quickly
EXCLAMATION

clamped their _____ over their mouths. They didn't
PART OF THE BODY (PLURAL)

want the counselor to _____ them!
VERB

The counselor placed his _____ hat over Wanda's face.
ADJECTIVE

Instantly, her body went limp like a dead _____. Leon
ANIMAL

screamed again.

"Good morning, _____," the lunch lady said over the
PLURAL NOUN

loudspeakers. The sound of her _____ voice woke up the rest
ADJECTIVE

of the campers. "_____ are ready in the mess hall!"
TYPE OF FOOD (PLURAL)

The morning _____ rang for breakfast.
NOUN

From TALES FROM MAD LIBS®: NIGHTMARE AT CAMP SMELLY LAKE
Copyright © 2019 by Penguin Random House LLC.

MAD LIBS® is fun to play with friends, but you can also play it by yourself! To begin with, DO NOT look at the chapter on the next page. Fill in the blanks on this page with the words called for. Then, using the words you have selected, fill in the blank spaces in the chapter.

Now you've created your own hilarious MAD LIBS® game!

CHAPTER 11: NIGHTMARE IN THE MEDICAL WARD

VERB _____

NUMBER _____

PART OF THE BODY (PLURAL) _____

TYPE OF LIQUID _____

ADVERB _____

SILLY WORD _____

ADJECTIVE _____

ADJECTIVE _____

PART OF THE BODY _____

NOUN _____

COLOR _____

SAME SILLY WORD _____

VERB _____

ADJECTIVE _____

ADJECTIVE _____

COLOR _____

PART OF THE BODY _____

CHAPTER 11:
NIGHTMARE IN THE MEDICAL WARD

Wanda opened her eyes and tried to _____ around.
<u>VERB</u>

She looked down to see _____ tubes connected to her
<u>NUMBER</u>

_____, pumping what looked like _____ .
<u>PART OF THE BODY (PLURAL)</u> <u>TYPE OF LIQUID</u>

"What day is it?" she said _____ to herself. "Where am I?!"
<u>ADVERB</u>

"It's _____ day," a cheerful voice said. "And you're in the
<u>SILLY WORD</u>

Medical Ward, the most _____ cabin at Camp _____
<u>ADJECTIVE</u> <u>ADJECTIVE</u>

Lake."

Wanda lifted her _____ and turned to the voice. A nurse
<u>PART OF THE BODY</u>

sat on a/an _____ in the corner of the room. The nurse
<u>NOUN</u>

chuckled and smoothed her _____ uniform.
<u>COLOR</u>

"Do you know what we do on _____ day, Wanda?" Wanda
<u>SAME SILLY WORD</u>

didn't know what to _____ .
<u>VERB</u>

"It all depends," the nurse continued. "Are you a/an _____
<u>ADJECTIVE</u>

patient? Or a/an _____ patient?"
<u>ADJECTIVE</u>

The nurse took off her _____ nursing cap and revealed her
<u>COLOR</u>

terrifying third _____ .
<u>PART OF THE BODY</u>

MAD LIBS® is fun to play with friends, but you can also play it by yourself! To begin with, DO NOT look at the chapter on the next page. Fill in the blanks on this page with the words called for. Then, using the words you have selected, fill in the blank spaces in the chapter.

Now you've created your own hilarious MAD LIBS® game!

CHAPTER 12: CRAFTY CORNER CONUNDRUMS

PLURAL NOUN _____

PART OF THE BODY (PLURAL) _____

NOUN _____

ADVERB _____

VERB ENDING IN "ING" _____

ADJECTIVE _____

ADJECTIVE _____

COLOR _____

ADJECTIVE _____

NOUN _____

COLOR _____

NOUN _____

PLURAL NOUN _____

ADJECTIVE _____

CHAPTER 12:
CRAFTY CORNER CONUNDRUMS

Meanwhile, Natasha and Leon were in the Craft Corner Cabin making

friendship bracelets. "How can we stop these _____ if they
                                              PLURAL NOUN

have _____ coming out of their heads?!" Leon asked.
     PART OF THE BODY (PLURAL)

"We just have to have a plan," Natasha said. Leon tied a/an _____
                                                              NOUN

to his bracelet and jingled his wrist.

"Hey!" he said _____ . "The other night, I saw a counselor
                  ADVERB

_____ toward the ancient _____ grounds."
VERB ENDING IN "ING"   ADJECTIVE

Natasha shuddered just thinking about that _____ night.
                                             ADJECTIVE

"That's where the groundskeeper said the creatures come from," she

replied, grabbing more _____ beads.
                        COLOR

"Are you sure we can trust that _____ old man? How do we
                                 ADJECTIVE

know he's not some type of _____ , too?" Leon asked. The craft
                            NOUN

counselor scratched under her _____ hat. Natasha flinched.
                               COLOR

The camp loudspeaker cut through the silence like a/an _____ .
                                                        NOUN

"Attention, _____ !" a counselor said. "The Safety Squad is
             PLURAL NOUN

doing an investigation. Which means, it's time to go camping near the

_____ burial grounds!"
ADJECTIVE

From TALES FROM MAD LIBS®: NIGHTMARE AT CAMP SMELLY LAKE
Copyright © 2019 by Penguin Random House LLC.

MAD LIBS® is fun to play with friends, but you can also play it by yourself! To begin with, DO NOT look at the chapter on the next page. Fill in the blanks on this page with the words called for. Then, using the words you have selected, fill in the blank spaces in the chapter.

Now you've created your own hilarious MAD LIBS® game!

CHAPTER 13:
A-HIKING WE WILL GO!

PLURAL NOUN _____

NUMBER _____

PLURAL NOUN _____

VERB _____

SILLY WORD _____

NOUN _____

TYPE OF LIQUID _____

COLOR _____

TYPE OF FOOD _____

ADVERB _____

VERB ENDING IN "ING" _____

FIRST NAME _____

ADJECTIVE _____

ADJECTIVE _____

CHAPTER 13:
A-HIKING WE WILL GO!

"I don't wanna camp near the ancient burial _____!"
_____ PLURAL NOUN

Leon squeaked.

"You couldn't pay me _____ dollars to do that!" Natasha said.
_____ NUMBER

"You heard the announcement, _____," the craft counselor
_____ PLURAL NOUN

said. "We're going camping! Or would you two rather _____ in
_____ VERB

Camp _____ Lake again?"
____ SILLY WORD

Natasha and Leon shot each other panicked looks and exited the

_____.
____ NOUN

Outside, the lunch lady was passing out bottles of _____
_____ TYPE OF LIQUID

and packs of _____ _____.
___ COLOR _____ TYPE OF FOOD

"Get yer food, kids!" she said _____.
_____ ADVERB

Leon slurped his drink and asked, "Which way are we

_____ to the campgrounds?"
_____ VERB ENDING IN "ING"

A counselor named _____ stared at Leon. "We head
_____ FIRST NAME

toward those _____ hills," she answered in a trance. Leon,
_____ ADJECTIVE

Natasha, and the rest of the _____ campers followed the
_____ ADJECTIVE

counselor toward the hills.

MAD LIBS® is fun to play with friends, but you can also play it by yourself! To begin with, DO NOT look at the chapter on the next page. Fill in the blanks on this page with the words called for. Then, using the words you have selected, fill in the blank spaces in the chapter.

Now you've created your own hilarious MAD LIBS® game!

CHAPTER 14:
CANOEING CAMP-OFF!

NOUN _____

ADJECTIVE _____

ADJECTIVE _____

ADJECTIVE _____

VERB ENDING IN "ING" _____

NOUN _____

ADJECTIVE _____

VERB _____

VERB _____

PART OF THE BODY _____

PLURAL NOUN _____

NOUN _____

COLOR _____

PLURAL NOUN _____

NOUN _____

VERB _____

CHAPTER 14:
CANOEING CAMP-OFF!

Natasha was out of breath when they reached the top of the

_____ . "Hurry up, Leon!" she yelled. "This view is _____."
　　NOUN　　　　　　　　　　　　　　　　　　　　　　ADJECTIVE

The top of the hill overlooked a/an _____ gorge with
　　　　　　　　　　　　　　　　　　ADJECTIVE

a/an _____ river running through it. Campers were carefully
　　　ADJECTIVE

_____ down the side of the gorge using a lengthy
VERB ENDING IN "ING"

_____ to guide them. "How the heck are we supposed to get
　　NOUN

to the ancient _____ grounds from here?" Leon asked.
　　　　　　　ADJECTIVE

"Looks like we have to _____ down this gorge and _____
　　　　　　　　　　　VERB　　　　　　　　　　　　　VERB

by canoe," Natasha said between breaths. She pointed with her

_____ to the river's edge, where counselors waited with
PART OF THE BODY

_____ near the water.
　PLURAL NOUN

"Well, this should be interesting," Leon said as he climbed down the

_____ . The two friends climbed into a canoe painted bright
　　NOUN

_____ . Natasha and Leon dipped their _____
　COLOR　　　　　　　　　　　　　　　　　　　　　　　　PLURAL NOUN

into the water and started paddling as fast as they could. "Wait just

one _____," Leon said. "Where did all of our counselors
　　　NOUN

_____ ?"
　VERB

MAD LIBS® is fun to play with friends, but you can also play it by yourself! To begin with, DO NOT look at the chapter on the next page. Fill in the blanks on this page with the words called for. Then, using the words you have selected, fill in the blank spaces in the chapter.

Now you've created your own hilarious MAD LIBS® game!

CHAPTER 15:
ROARING RIVER MADNESS

VERB _____

PLURAL NOUN _____

ADJECTIVE _____

VERB (PAST TENSE) _____

EXCLAMATION _____

VERB _____

NOUN _____

ADJECTIVE _____

NOUN _____

NOUN _____

NOUN _____

PLURAL NOUN _____

VERB _____

ADJECTIVE _____

PLURAL NOUN _____

CHAPTER 15:
ROARING RIVER MADNESS

"I don't _____ any of the counselors anywhere!" Leon yelled
      VERB

from the back of the canoe.

"I can't tell which is scarier: those spooky _____ or these
                                                   PLURAL NOUN

_____ rapids!" Natasha gulped. A wave _____ against
ADJECTIVE   VERB (PAST TENSE)

their canoe and pushed the friends dangerously close to the rocks.

"_____!" Natasha yelled, paddling against the current.
   EXCLAMATION

Suddenly, Natasha felt something slimy _____ her arm.
                                         VERB

"Watch out, Natasha!" Leon yelled, and let out a blood-curdling

_____. A/An _____ creature was clinging to the side
NOUN   ADJECTIVE

of their _____, trying to climb on board.
         NOUN

"They're in the water!" Natasha screamed, smacking at the

_____ with her oar. "The counselors, or whatever, are hiding
NOUN

in the _____!" The rest of the campers screamed as more and
        NOUN

more _____ appeared in the water. A second-year camper
     PLURAL NOUN

tried to _____ a creature, but the creature threw her into the
       VERB

_____ water. Natasha and Leon paddled away like their
ADJECTIVE

_____ depended on it.
PLURAL NOUN

MAD LIBS® is fun to play with friends, but you can also play it by yourself! To begin with, DO NOT look at the chapter on the next page. Fill in the blanks on this page with the words called for. Then, using the words you have selected, fill in the blank spaces in the chapter.

Now you've created your own hilarious MAD LIBS® game!

CHAPTER 16: BURIED BONES

NUMBER _____

NOUN _____

NOUN _____

ADJECTIVE _____

ADJECTIVE _____

ADJECTIVE _____

PLURAL NOUN _____

PLURAL NOUN _____

NOUN _____

COLOR _____

TYPE OF FOOD _____

LAST NAME _____

ADJECTIVE _____

PART OF THE BODY (PLURAL) _____

ADJECTIVE _____

PART OF THE BODY (PLURAL) _____

NOUN _____

CHAPTER 16:
BURIED BONES

After paddling for _____ minutes, Natasha and Leon reached
                    NUMBER

a bend in the _____ . They pulled their _____ to the
              NOUN   NOUN

shore and walked along the riverbank. "We must be near the ancient

_____ grounds," Natasha said. It was night and the sky was
ADJECTIVE

_____ . The friends stood on a/an _____ beach
ADJECTIVE   ADJECTIVE

covered in _____ and bones.
           PLURAL NOUN

"These _____ don't look so ancient to me . . . ," Leon said.
       PLURAL NOUN

"Oh my _____ , Leon! What's over there?" Natasha pulled
        NOUN

out a/an _____ trophy stuck in between some muddy rocks.
         COLOR

"It's the championship trophy for the greased _____
                                              TYPE OF FOOD

tournament!" she said. "Winner, 1981. A. _____ . Who's that?"
                                          LAST NAME

"A for Amanda," a/an _____ voice said.
                     ADJECTIVE

Natasha and Leon couldn't believe their _____ .
                                        PART OF THE BODY (PLURAL)

Wanda stepped out from the darkness. A small _____ growth
                                             ADJECTIVE

was protruding from her head, and medical tubes hung from her

_____ . "I escaped the Medical _____ ,"
PART OF THE BODY (PLURAL)   NOUN

Wanda explained. "We gotta get out of here, or you're next!"

MAD LIBS® is fun to play with friends, but you can also play it by yourself! To begin with, DO NOT look at the chapter on the next page. Fill in the blanks on this page with the words called for. Then, using the words you have selected, fill in the blank spaces in the chapter.

Now you've created your own hilarious MAD LIBS® game!

CHAPTER 17: BOG BEGINNINGS

PART OF THE BODY _____

COLOR _____

ADJECTIVE _____

PART OF THE BODY (PLURAL) _____

FIRST NAME _____

ADJECTIVE _____

ADJECTIVE _____

ADJECTIVE _____

TYPE OF LIQUID _____

VERB _____

COLOR _____

NUMBER _____

NOUN _____

ANIMAL _____

COLOR _____

ADVERB _____

CHAPTER 17: BOG BEGINNINGS

Wanda patted the _____ that was growing out of her
                    PART OF THE BODY

forehead. It glowed _____ . She sighed. "This way," Wanda
                        COLOR

said, and shuffled farther into the _____ woods. Leon linked
                                        ADJECTIVE

_____ with Natasha and followed.
PART OF THE BODY (PLURAL)

"I can't believe my Uncle _____ allowed me to come to
                              FIRST NAME

this _____ camp," he whispered.
        ADJECTIVE

Slurp! Slop! Thup!

"EWWWWWWW!" Natasha yelled. "The ground is _____
                                                  ADJECTIVE

and mucky," she said. "My feet are all _____ now!"
                                          ADJECTIVE

The campers walked into a giant puddle of _____ .
                                              TYPE OF LIQUID

"Does anyone have a flashlight?" Leon asked, not sure if he wanted

to _____ what was in front of him. Wanda's forehead glowed
      VERB

_____ and brightened their path. They were wading in
  COLOR

_____ feet of water in the middle of a bog. Ahead of them, a
  NUMBER

creature that looked like the lunch _____ was chewing on a
                                        NOUN

dead _____ . The creature's eyes glowed _____ as it
        ANIMAL   COLOR

dropped the meat and belched. _____ , the creature attacked!
                                  ADVERB

MAD LIBS® is fun to play with friends, but you can also play it by yourself! To begin with, DO NOT look at the chapter on the next page. Fill in the blanks on this page with the words called for. Then, using the words you have selected, fill in the blank spaces in the chapter.

Now you've created your own hilarious MAD LIBS® game!

CHAPTER 18:
A LUCKY SHOT

EXCLAMATION _____

VERB _____

PART OF THE BODY _____

VERB (PAST TENSE) _____

VERB _____

PLURAL NOUN _____

PART OF THE BODY (PLURAL) _____

ADJECTIVE _____

VERB _____

COLOR _____

ADJECTIVE _____

ADJECTIVE _____

TYPE OF LIQUID _____

ADJECTIVE _____

CHAPTER 18:
A LUCKY SHOT

"_____!" screamed Leon, as the creature began to
　　EXCLAMATION

_____ on his _____. The creature growled and
　VERB　　　　　　　PART OF THE BODY

_____ hungrily. Natasha and Wanda tried to _____
VERB (PAST TENSE)　　　　　　　　　　　　　　　　　　　　VERB

the creature away with _____ they found floating in the
　　　　　　　　　　　PLURAL NOUN

bog, but Leon could not escape.

Thump!

Suddenly, the creature was hit between its _____
　　　　　　　　　　　　　　　　　　　PART OF THE BODY (PLURAL)

and fell down. Its _____ body bobbed up and down in the bog.
　　　　　　　ADJECTIVE

"Nice shot, Natasha!" Leon said.

"I didn't _____ that," Natasha said, bewildered.
　　　　　VERB

"Me neither," Wanda said, rubbing her forehead, which was quickly

turning _____ .
　　　　COLOR

"Just a lucky shot, I guess," a/an _____ voice said behind
　　　　　　　　　　　　　　　　ADJECTIVE

them.

The campers spun around to see the _____ groundskeeper
　　　　　　　　　　　　　　　　　ADJECTIVE

wading in the _____ behind them. "There's no time," he
　　　　　TYPE OF LIQUID

said. "Follow me if you want to make it out of here _____!"
　　　　　　　　　　　　　　　　　　　　　　　　　ADJECTIVE

MAD LIBS® is fun to play with friends, but you can also play it by yourself! To begin with, DO NOT look at the chapter on the next page. Fill in the blanks on this page with the words called for. Then, using the words you have selected, fill in the blank spaces in the chapter.

Now you've created your own hilarious MAD LIBS® game!

CHAPTER 19:
PEDAL TO THE METAL

PART OF THE BODY _____

NOUN _____

COLOR _____

NOUN _____

VERB (PAST TENSE) _____

PART OF THE BODY _____

VERB _____

PART OF THE BODY (PLURAL) _____

ANIMAL _____

NOUN _____

ADJECTIVE _____

ADJECTIVE _____

NUMBER _____

VERB _____

ADJECTIVE _____

PART OF THE BODY _____

CHAPTER 19:
PEDAL TO THE METAL

With flashlight in _____, the groundskeeper led the
PART OF THE BODY

campers out of the bog. When they reached the edge of the _____,
NOUN

they scrambled toward his _____ pickup truck. "Get in!" said
COLOR

the old man, hopping in the driver's _____ .
NOUN

"You're gonna be all right, Leon," Natasha said. She helped Leon into

the bed of the truck and _____ in beside him. Wanda
VERB (PAST TENSE)

and her glowing _____ followed.
PART OF THE BODY

"We gotta _____ through the hills," the old man shouted.
VERB

"*They* can't climb with their webbed _____."
PART OF THE BODY (PLURAL)

The truck's engine roared to life like a/an _____ . The old
ANIMAL

man stepped on the gas _____ and sped off into the night. As
NOUN

the truck barreled up the _____ hill, a creature lurched into
ADJECTIVE

the truck bed! It opened its _____ mouth, baring _____
ADJECTIVE   NUMBER

sharp teeth.

"It's going to _____ me!" Leon wailed. The creature stood
VERB

up _____ and tall. A tree branch slapped its _____ ,
ADJECTIVE   PART OF THE BODY

and the creature was knocked out of the truck. The truck sped away.

MAD LIBS® is fun to play with friends, but you can also play it by yourself! To begin with, DO NOT look at the chapter on the next page. Fill in the blanks on this page with the words called for. Then, using the words you have selected, fill in the blank spaces in the chapter.

Now you've created your own hilarious MAD LIBS® game!

CHAPTER 20:
THE COUNSELORS SPEAK

COLOR _____

ADJECTIVE _____

ADJECTIVE _____

ADJECTIVE _____

NUMBER _____

PART OF THE BODY (PLURAL) _____

COLOR _____

PART OF THE BODY _____

PLURAL NOUN _____

ADJECTIVE _____

NOUN _____

EXCLAMATION _____

PLURAL NOUN _____

CHAPTER 20:
THE COUNSELORS SPEAK

The bright _____ beams of the groundskeeper's headlights
                    COLOR

illuminated the main yard of Camp _____ Lake.
                                        ADJECTIVE

"Hold tight! We need to drive through the camp and back onto the

_____ road," the groundskeeper hollered.
ADJECTIVE

Suddenly, _____ figures emerged from the darkness,
              ADJECTIVE

blocking their path. The groundskeeper brought the truck to a halt. All

_____ of the counselors were standing in the middle of the yard,
NUMBER

their third _____ glowing _____ . Wanda
              PART OF THE BODY (PLURAL)   COLOR

touched her _____ to her forehead and groaned.
              PART OF THE BODY

"Never fear, _____ ," the counselors said in unison. "The
                PLURAL NOUN

Safety Squad is here!" The counselors bared their _____ teeth
                                                      ADJECTIVE

and lunged toward the truck.

"Let's get the _____ out of here!" Natasha screamed as she,
                  NOUN

Leon, and Wanda ran from the truck.

"_____ !" they heard the groundskeeper cry.
  EXCLAMATION

"He's a goner!" Natasha shouted. "We need to hide or the

_____ will get us, too!"
PLURAL NOUN

MAD LIBS® is fun to play with friends, but you can also play it by yourself! To begin with, DO NOT look at the chapter on the next page. Fill in the blanks on this page with the words called for. Then, using the words you have selected, fill in the blank spaces in the chapter.

Now you've created your own hilarious MAD LIBS® game!

CHAPTER 21: HIDE-AND-SEEK

ANIMAL _____

NOUN _____

ADJECTIVE _____

PLURAL NOUN _____

NOUN _____

ADVERB _____

PLURAL NOUN _____

VERB _____

PLURAL NOUN _____

ADJECTIVE _____

VERB ENDING IN "ING" _____

NOUN _____

PART OF THE BODY (PLURAL) _____

ADJECTIVE _____

COLOR _____

NOUN _____

CHAPTER 21:
HIDE-AND-SEEK

"It smells like a rotting _____ in here," Leon said as Natasha
                              ANIMAL

opened the door to the Craft Corner _____ .
                                        NOUN

"Safe and smelly is better than dead and _____ ," Natasha said.
                                              ADJECTIVE

"We can use these _____ to board up the windows and doors."
                      PLURAL NOUN

They stepped inside, and Natasha shut the _____ . "We need to
                                               NOUN

move _____ . Wanda, grab a hammer and some _____ ,"
        ADVERB   PLURAL NOUN

Natasha said. "Leon, help me _____ these windows."
                                  VERB

Leon found some _____ in a box and got to work. Suddenly,
                    PLURAL NOUN

Natasha heard a/an _____ noise.
                       ADJECTIVE

"Leon? Is your stomach _____ ?" Natasha asked.
                           VERB ENDING IN "ING"

"That's not me," Leon said. Natasha whirled around and screamed

bloody _____ .
            NOUN

"W-W-Wanda?" she said. "What big _____ you
                                      PART OF THE BODY (PLURAL)

have!" Leon squealed and ran toward Natasha. Wanda bared her

_____ teeth at Leon and Natasha. Then, everything went
   ADJECTIVE

_____ .
   COLOR

The _____
        NOUN

From TALES FROM MAD LIBS®: NIGHTMARE AT CAMP SMELLY LAKE
Copyright © 2019 by Penguin Random House LLC.

Join the millions of Mad Libs fans creating wacky and wonderful stories on our apps!

Download Mad Libs today!